The Progressive Movement 19[...]
Efforts to Reform America's Ne[...]

FIGHTING RACIAL DISCRIMINATION
Treating All Americans Fairly Under the Law

Wayne Anderson

The Rosen Publishing Group, Inc., New York

To Robbie, for helping me realize that I can go home again.

Published in 2006 by The Rosen Publishing Group, Inc.
29 East 21st Street, New York, NY 10010

Copyright © 2006 by The Rosen Publishing Group, Inc.

First Edition

All rights reserved. No part of this book may be reproduced in any form without permission in writing from the publisher, except by a reviewer.

Library of Congress Cataloging-in-Publication Data
Anderson, Wayne, 1966–
Fighting racial discrimination : treating all Americans fairly under the law / by Wayne Anderson.
   p. cm. — (The Progressive movement 1900–1920: efforts to reform America's new industrial society)
Includes bibliographical references and index.
ISBN 1-4042-0189-0 (lib. bdg.)
ISBN 1-4042-0847-X (pbk. bdg.)
6-pack ISBN 1-4042-6187-7
1. African Americans—Civil rights—History—20th century—Juvenile literature. 2. African Americans—Legal status, laws, etc.—History—20th century—Juvenile literature. 3. Race discrimination—United States—History—20th century—Juvenile literature. 4. Race discrimination—Law and legislation—United States—History—20th century—Juvenile literature. 5. United States—Race relations—Juvenile literature. 6. United States—Politics and government—1901–1953—Juvenile literature. 7. Progressivism (United States politics)—Juvenile literature. I. Title. II. Series.
E185.61.A57 2004
323.173—dc22

2004000751

Manufactured in the United States of America

On the cover: Top: African American dwelling, Georgia, circa 1900. Bottom: Silent protest parade in New York City to protest the East St. Louis riots, 1917.

Photo credits: Cover (top) © Photo Collection Alexander Alland, Sr./Corbis; cover (bottom), pp. 5, 6, 13 Library of Congress Prints and Photographs Division; p. 8 © Private Collection/Bridgeman Art Library; p. 10 National Archives; p. 12 © Corbis; p. 15 © Hulton Archive/Getty Images; p. 16 Chicago Historical Society; pp. 19, 25 General Research Division, The New York Public Library, Astor, Lenox, and Tilden Foundations; p. 21 Courtesy of the Illinois State Historical Library; pp. 22 (top), 27 (left) Photographs and Prints Division, Schomburg Center for Research in Black Culture, The New York Public Library, Astor, Lenox, and Tilden Foundations; p. 22 (bottom) Library of Congress, NAACP Collection, Manuscript Division; p. 27 (right) © Bettmann/Corbis.

Designer: Les Kanturek; Editor: Mark Beyer; Photo Researcher: Amy Feinberg

Contents

Chapter One   The Progressive Era
and Segregation 4

Chapter Two   Coping with Segregation 11

Chapter Three   The Response
of Progressives 18

Chapter Four   The NAACP at Work 24

Glossary 29
Web Sites 30
Primary Source Image List ... 30
Index 31

Chapter One

The Progressive Era and Segregation

The Progressive Era took place in the United States between 1900 and 1920. During these years, many important political, economic, and social reforms took place. These reforms came from hard work by common people who wanted change for everyone. These people were known as political activists. They called themselves Progressives.

Most of the Progressives worked to end some of the problems that had started during the second half of the nineteenth century. These problems included the rapid industrialization of the country. This brought many thousands of people from the countryside into cities to work in factories. Such a fast change caused urbanization, a quick rise in the populations of cities. The need to fill all these jobs caused a huge increase in immigration during the same time.

Cities grew around factories that needed thousands of workers. People lived in crowded and unsafe conditions. This is a map of Birmingham, Alabama, in 1885. In the South, though, blacks were shut out of many jobs that could have helped their lives.

Each of these events caused problems for people. New laws needed to be passed to protect people, businesses, and the factories and cities in which they worked and lived. Those who helped pass such laws included private citizens, church and community leaders, members of the

Even with industrial growth, people lost their jobs. Progressives wanted to stop big businesses from taking over small businesses and putting people out of work. People began to protest for workers' rights.

media, and politicians. Each of these groups or individuals worked at the local, state, and national levels to fix the problems they found. Some of these problems included dangerous working conditions in factories. Others included poor living conditions and discrimination against immigrants and minorities.

Some reformers worked to change what they regarded as social wrongs that harmed all of society. One of these wrongs was racial segregation (keeping blacks and whites apart). Progressives worked to expose the horrors of segregation. To fight back, they formed the National Association for the Advancement of Colored People (NAACP).

The history of African Americans up to the Progressive Era had been one of slavery and segregation. Between the mid-1700s and 1865, most of the black people in the United States lived in the South and worked as slaves. For much of that time, people in the North argued with those in the South over whether slavery should be allowed in the United States. This disagreement helped begin the Civil War in 1861.

When the Civil War ended in 1865, the North had won. Slavery was quickly abolished, or ended forever. At the time, Congress was filled with lawmakers from the Northern states. Congress passed a number of laws against

Plantations in the South used slaves to work the land. This made their owners rich, but gave nothing to the black slaves. After slavery ended in 1865, blacks were free, but still suffered discrimination.

discrimination. It also made several constitutional amendments aimed at guaranteeing the civil rights of African Americans.

However, the Southern states did not cooperate. Almost immediately, the South made a group of laws known as the black codes. The black codes enforced segregation by limiting the freedoms of the former slaves. Some laws made it illegal for blacks to live in many places. Other laws kept former slaves from being able to find work. Congress struck down the black codes under Reconstruction. Reconstruction was a program for reunifying (making whole again) the country after the Civil War. When Reconstruction ended in 1877, the Southern states simply made up new laws against the blacks. These became known as Jim Crow laws.

Some blacks challenged the laws in court. One case asked the court system to decide if a Louisiana law followed the U.S. Constitution. If the law did not, then it would be struck down. If the court found the law was just, then it could still be used. The law in question ordered separate cars for whites and blacks on passenger trains operating within Louisiana. This case was argued all the way to the U.S. Supreme Court. In 1896, it was tried before the Supreme Court under the name *Plessy v. Ferguson*. The Supreme Court said that it was OK for states to separate blacks and whites on their railroads. All the railroads had to ensure was that rail cars and service were equal for both groups.

The Supreme Court decision in *Plessy v. Ferguson* had a bad effect on the lives of African Americans. The Southern

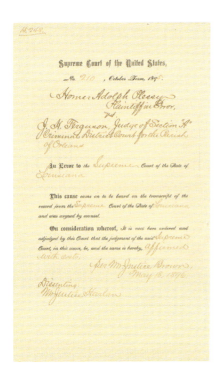

The 1896 U.S. Supreme Court decision in *Plessy v. Ferguson* made it legal to separate the white and black races. The case came from a Louisiana law forcing blacks to use separate railroad cars from whites.

states almost immediately passed more Jim Crow laws to enforce segregation in other areas of public life. Before *Plessy v. Ferguson*, the accommodations for blacks, where they were given, were worse than those set aside for whites. Segregation became a way of life, even in many areas of the North. In many instances, no law was required to enforce it.

Chapter Two

Coping with Segregation

Segregation affected almost every part of African American life. It followed blacks from the time they were born until the time they were buried. Just about everything was segregated—hospitals, churches, schools, restaurants, restrooms, buses, and even cemeteries. In the few places used by both races, blacks were forced to stand aside and wait until all the whites were served. They also had to wait to be first addressed by the salesperson. In addition, the Southern states, by law and by custom, set up obstacles to prevent blacks from using their constitutional rights. These included acts such as voting and serving on juries.

The Jim Crow laws were strongly put into action. Blacks who dared to use "whites only" places or services risked being fined, imprisoned, or beaten by a mob. Sometimes blacks were murdered for their actions.

The decades following the freedom of slaves saw many black men lynched by whites. This did not happen only in the South. This photo shows a crowd of white men in 1882 in Minneapolis, Minnesota, watching the hanging of a black man.

Lynching, or mob execution, especially by hanging, became a common punishment for black men accused of committing a crime. To make matters worse, most blacks depended on whites for work or were tied up in one-sided land-rental agreements known as sharecropping.

Therefore, openly challenging the laws could make it impossible for a black to earn an income.

All this served to keep blacks in a lower position than whites. This was the aim behind the laws in the first place. White Southerners who were angry about the negative effect that the abolition of slavery had on their way of life sought to keep blacks in a position as close to slavery as possible.

It was not easy for blacks to live under such conditions. For most, there was the ever-present fear of being seen as breaking the code. Most coped by simply avoiding contact with whites as much as possible. When they came into contact with whites, they usually acted in a submissive and obeying way, holding their heads down and avoiding eye contact. Many moved to the North where the treatment of blacks was not as severe and where job prospects were better.

Many blacks started businesses to fill the needs of their communities. These usually included grocery stores,

Other forms of discrimination came in outright refusal to serve blacks in stores and restaurants. Many businesses had signs in their windows telling blacks that they were not wanted.

funeral parlors, barbershops, beauty parlors, and social clubs. Black churches often doubled as community centers. Churches also helped in setting up schools, banks, insurance companies, and volunteer fire departments. Black-owned newspapers reported news not covered in the larger, white-owned newspapers. These papers celebrated the achievements of African Americans and gave voice to their suffering.

Many blacks fought hard against the Jim Crow laws. Individuals made acts of defiance at the risk of being arrested, losing a job, or being lynched. Others formed groups that organized boycotts of white stores, challenged laws in court, and petitioned Congress to put an end to segregation. Black churches and newspapers spread news of resistance activities and triumphs to other neighborhoods in the South. These success stories eventually made it to the North. Journalists wrote stories and editorials condemning segregation, lynching, and court decisions and new laws that were unfavorable to blacks.

One of the most outspoken black journalists was Ida B. Wells. One evening in 1892, three black men were lynched in Memphis, Tennessee. Afterward, Ida B. Wells lashed out against the city in a series of articles in the *Memphis Free Speech*. Angry whites destroyed her newspaper. She was forced to leave Memphis. But she refused to be silenced. She moved to Chicago, where she carried on her anti-lynching campaign. Between 1892 and 1900, she wrote a number of pamphlets. The first was titled *Southern Horrors: Lynch Law in All Its Phases*.

Journalist Ida B. Wells made public the discrimination blacks suffered throughout the United States. Her pamphlets urged people to take notice of this nationwide problem.

Around the turn of the twentieth century, two other African Americans rose to national prominence. Their approach to segregation could not have been more different. The first, Booker T. Washington, was an educator and founder of the Tuskegee Institute in Alabama. Tuskegee focused on teaching African Americans trade skills. In a famous speech in Atlanta, Georgia, in 1895, Washington urged blacks to focus on opportunities rather than grievances. He argued for a new way in which blacks could gain rights and freedoms in the United States. Washington wanted blacks to accept their place in society while trying to gain the trust of whites through education and economic self-reliance.

15

Booker T. Washington preached acceptance to blacks. He wanted to help the members of the black community make their lives better through education and working. Whites liked Washington, while many black-rights advocates opposed his views.

These views made Washington popular with whites. They looked at him as the main spokesperson for blacks. The success of Tuskegee and his larger-than-life personality made Washington a leader among African Americans. Washington became arguably the most powerful black man in the United States. Two presidents, Theodore Roosevelt and William Howard Taft, often turned to him for advice about African American issues.

The other famous black-rights advocate was writer and professor W. E. B. DuBois. DuBois publicly and bitterly disagreed with Washington. He rejected Washington's approach. DuBois argued that letting whites get away with their treatment of blacks would only serve to prolong the oppression of African Americans. In his famous book *The Souls of Black Folk* (1903), he documented the terrible conditions under which African Americans lived. He called for immediate and complete racial equality. In 1905, he invited a group of black professionals to form the Niagara Movement, an organization to confront white racism.

Chapter Three

The Response of Progressives

Few Progressives spent much time trying to put an end to segregation. However, those who did worked hard to get the troubles of African Americans on the national agenda.

Ray Stannard Baker was one of the first Progressives to pick up the cause. Baker was a muckraker. Muckrakers were newspaper and magazine writers who went around the country exposing political and corporate corruption. Muckrakers also wrote about social ills. Muckrakers were very important to the Progressive movement because their articles and books raised public awareness and outcry. This made it easier for the reformers to push for new laws.

Between 1906 and the mid-1910s, Baker wrote many articles about America's racial divide. In an article called "What Is a Lynching?" published in *McClure's Magazine* in February 1905, he described in detail a lynching he had

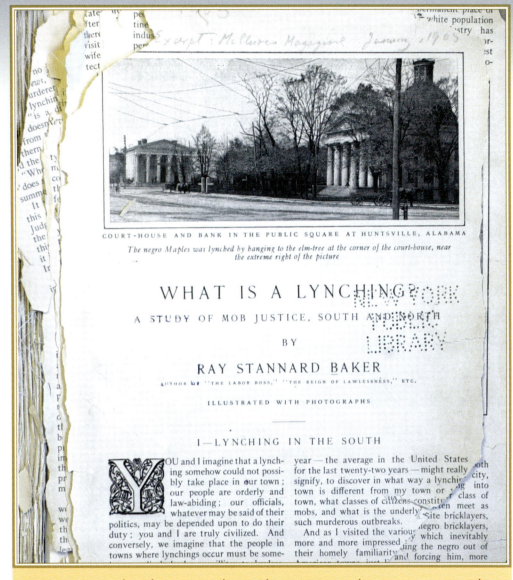

Ray Stannard Baker's article "What Is a Lynching?" appeared in the national publication *McClure's Magazine* in 1905. Baker described the horror he felt when he witnessed a lynching. Articles on discrimination and segregation gave rise to greater knowledge that the government needed to do something to help African Americans.

seen in Springfield, Ohio. He wrote, "They murdered the Negro in cold blood in the jail doorway; then they dragged him to the principal business street and hung him to a telegraph-pole, afterward riddling his lifeless body with revolver shots."

In a famous series of articles called "Following the Color Line," published in *American Magazine* in 1908, Baker showed how racism and segregation blanketed the country. Although Baker's work did not lead to laws outlawing segregation, he called greater attention to the situation and convinced many people in the North that they, too, were part of the problem.

On August 14, 1908, reports that a black man had raped a white woman led to a race riot in Springfield, Illinois. At first, an angry white mob went to the jail to lynch the suspect. When they did not find him there, they marched through the black section of the town to take revenge on its residents. The riot lasted five days and was finally put down by soldiers. At the end of the riot, two blacks and four whites had been killed. Forty black families lost their homes to fires set by the mob.

A month after the riot, William English Walling, a white Southern journalist, ran an article in the *Independent*. He pointed out that the race-baiting, or name calling, that took

The riots of August 14, 1908, in Springfield, Illinois, showed how bad relations had gotten between whites and blacks. Soldiers had to stop the fighting between the two groups living side by side in Illinois's capital city.

place in Illinois could happen anywhere in America. He asked, "Who realizes the seriousness of the situation . . . What large and powerful body of citizens is ready to come to the Negro's aid?" as quoted in *Simple Justice* by Richard Kluger. Upon reading the article, a white social worker

African American groups around the country decided to act for themselves. A group of activists sent out a letter *(bottom)*, urging people to attend a conference to organize a national activist group. The result was the formation of the National Association for the Advancement of Colored People (NAACP). This activist group worked to change laws that favored whites and discriminated against blacks.

named Mary White Ovington wrote to Walling about starting such an organization. Together, they approached Oswald Garrison Villard, the powerful and wealthy editor of the *New York Evening Post*. Villard liked the idea and joined their efforts. The trio organized a conference to be held on May 31, 1909, and Villard issued what has come to be known as "the call," inviting interested persons to attend. Sixty white and black activists signed up for the conference. They included Jane Addams, one of the country's leading Progressives, W. E. B. DuBois, Ida B. Wells, and philosopher John Dewey.

The result of the conference, which was attended by about 300 people, was the formation of the National Association for the Advancement of Colored People (NAACP). Its stated goal was "to work toward the abolition of forced segregation, promotion of equal education and civil rights under the protection of law, and an end to race violence." Funded by and, at first, led by whites, the NAACP was the Progressives' main answer to the problem of segregation. It was the first national civil rights organization in the United States. William Walling served as the first chairman of its executive committee, of which DuBois, the director of publicity, was the only African American member.

Chapter Four

The NAACP at Work

The NAACP set up its national office in New York City in 1910. The group then quickly went to work challenging segregation. That year it joined the U.S. Supreme Court case of a black farmer named Pink Franklin. Franklin had killed a policeman in self-defense after the officer broke into his home in the middle of the night to arrest him. The case, which the NAACP lost, marked the beginning of a long legal battle against segregation.

In its next case, also in 1910, the NAACP helped to convince the Supreme Court to strike down an Oklahoma election law that made it difficult for blacks to vote. The organization won another major Supreme Court battle in 1917, when the Court ruled that a Louisville, Kentucky, law requiring blacks to live in certain sections of the city was unconstitutional. The NAACP participated in and

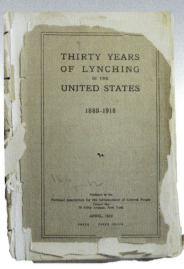

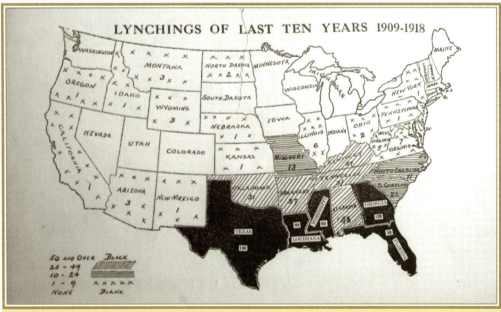

The NAACP worked in Washington, D.C., to get members of Congress to help African Americans. It published important documents, including this book *(top)*, a thirty-year history of lynching in the United States. In the book, maps showed the number of lynchings occurring throughout the country, state by state.

won many other court cases at the state and local level during the Progressive Era.

In addition to court cases, the NAACP became a powerful lobbying force. It launched huge public protests in 1913 when President Woodrow Wilson introduced segregation into the federal government and in 1915 when the racially offensive film *Birth of a Nation* was released. In 1917, it successfully lobbied (influenced) the federal government to allow blacks to be commissioned as officers in the army in World War I.

Although the association failed to get Congress to pass an anti-lynching law, it pressured President Wilson into making a public statement against lynching in 1918. The NAACP maintained a strong drive against lynching. In 1919, it published *Thirty Years of Lynching in the United States, 1889–1918*. This piece was a close look at lynching. Many NAACP leaders put their lives at risk investigating the stories behind the lynchings. In 1922, the NAACP began taking out large ads in major newspapers, presenting the ugly facts about such mob violence against blacks.

Through its efforts and successes, the NAACP grew rapidly. By 1914, it had 6,000 members and offices in fifty cities. Five years later, it had nearly 90,000 members in more than 300 branches (smaller groups). Circulation of

W. E. B. DuBois *(second from right, standing)* edited the NAACP journal *The Crisis*. This publication informed the public about the need for change in the country's laws. The cover shown here is from the first issue of the journal in November 1910.

The Crisis, the NAACP's journal that was edited by DuBois, rose from 1,000 copies in 1910 to 10,000 a year later and to 100,000 by 1920.

Despite the NAACP's achievements in its first ten years, many historians view the Progressive movement as having failed to tackle racial segregation. It is true that racial injustice was a low priority for whites and that some Progressives were motivated by their fears of the impact that blacks and new immigrants would have on traditional American values. Segregation actually grew worse during the Progressive Era. Most of the Progressive reforms took place in the urban North, while about 90 percent of the nation's African American citizens lived in the rural South. Moreover, as more blacks moved into Northern cities, the practice of discrimination, if not segregation laws, followed them.

On the other hand, it is also true that the formation of the NAACP laid the foundation for the civil rights triumphs of the mid- to late twentieth century. Most notable among these is the *Brown v. Board of Education* decision of 1954, in which the Supreme Court overturned the Jim Crow standard that was set in *Plessy v. Ferguson*. This victory gave boost to the civil rights movement of the 1960s, which yielded its own set of reforms that matched the drive and spirit of those of the Progressive Era.

Glossary

black codes (BLAK COHDZ) The set of laws passed in the South following the abolition of slavery that sought to control the movement and activities of former slaves.

civil rights (CIH-vuhl RYTZ) The basic nonpolitical rights belonging to citizens.

industrialization (ihn-duhs-trih-a-ly-ZAY-shun) When a society changes from being farm based to factory based.

Jim Crow laws (JIHM CROH LAWZ) Segregation laws that required racial separation.

lynching (LIHN-ching) Execution (especially by a mob), often by hanging, without due process of the law.

muckraker (MUHK-rayk-er) Journalist who writes about political and social problems in America.

petition (puh-TIH-shun) A legal or formal request.

Reconstruction (ree-cuhn-STRUHK-shun) The years 1865 to 1877, after the Civil War, dedicated to rebuilding the South and making laws for voting, civil rights, and trade.

segregation (sehg-rih-GAY-shun) The separation of people of different races, classes, or ethnic groups.

urbanization (er-buhn-eye-ZAY-shun) The development of a region into a city.

Web Sites

Due to the changing nature of Internet links, the Rosen Publishing Group, Inc., has developed an online list of Web sites related to the subject of this book. This site is updated regularly. Please use this link to access the list:

http://www.rosenlinks.com/pmnhnt/fird

Primary Source Image List

Cover: Top: African American residents pose in front of a shack in Georgia, circa 1900, by Alexander Alland. Bottom: Photographic print of silent protest parade in New York City, 1917, copyright by Underwood & Underwood, N.Y. Currently part of the Visual Materials collection from the National Association for the Advancement of Colored People Records.

Page 5: Lithograph of Birmingham, Alabama, created/published by Norris, Wellege & Co., 1885. Currently housed at the Library of Congress, Washington, D.C.

Page 6: Photograph of men picketing for jobs, May 31, 1909. Currently housed at the Library of Congress, Washington, D.C.

Page 8: Color lithograph of a Mississippi plantation, nineteenth century. Currently housed at the Museum of the City of New York.

Page 10: First page of *Plessy v. Ferguson* decision handed down by the U.S. Supreme Court, 1896.

Page 12: Photograph of lynching in Minneapolis, Minnesota, 1882, by H. R. Farr.

Page 13: Photograph of sign discrimination against blacks at Lancaster, Ohio, business, 1938, by Ben Shahn. Currently housed at the Library of Congress, Washington, D.C.

Page 15: Portrait of Ida Wells Barnett, circa 1890.

Page 16: Photograph of Booker T. Washington, 1911, by the *Chicago Daily News*. Currently housed at the Chicago Historical Society.

Page 19: Photograph of original page from Ray Stannard Baker's article "What Is a Lynching?" published in *McClure's Magazine*, February 1905. Currently housed at the New York Public Library.

Page 22: Top: Early members of the NAACP. Housed in the Photographs and Prints Division, Schomburg Center for Research in Black Culture, the New York Public Library. Bottom: Letter sent to organize meeting to establish the NAACP, February 6, 1909. Currently housed at the Library of Congress, Washington, D.C.

Page 25: Pages from *Thirty Years of Lynching in the United States, 1889–1918*, published by the NAACP, 1919.

Page 27: Left: portrait of the offices of *The Crisis*, circa 1911. Currently housed at the New York Public Library. Right: Cover of the first issue of *The Crisis*, November 1910.

Index

A
Addams, Jane, 23

B
Baker, Ray Stannard, 18–20
black codes, 9
Brown v. Board of Education, 28

C
civil rights, 8, 23, 28
Civil War, 7, 9
Congress, 7, 9, 14, 26
Constitution, U.S., 9

D
Dewey, John, 23
discrimination, 7, 8, 28
DuBois, W. E. B., 17, 23, 27

I
immigration/immigrants, 4, 7, 28

J
Jim Crow laws, 9, 10, 11, 14, 28

L
lynching, 12, 14, 15, 18, 26

M
muckrakers, 18

N
National Association for the Advancement of Colored People (NAACP), 7, 23, 24–27, 28
Niagara Movement, 17

P
Plessy v. Ferguson, 9, 10, 28
Progressive Era, 4, 7, 18, 26, 27, 28
Progressives, 4, 7, 18, 23, 27–28

R
racism, 17, 20
Reconstruction, 9
Roosevelt, Theodore, 17

S
segregation, 7, 9, 10, 11, 14, 15, 18, 20, 23, 24, 26, 27, 28
slavery/slaves, 7, 9, 13
Supreme Court cases, 9, 24, 28

T
Taft, William Howard, 17

W
Walling, William English, 20–23, 24
Washington, Booker T., 15–17
Wells, Ida B., 14–15, 23
Wilson, Woodrow, 26

About the Author

Wayne Anderson is a freelance writer and editor who lives in New York City. A native of Jamaica, he is a former music editor for the *New York Carib News*, the largest Caribbean American newsweekly in the United States, and the author of four books for young adults. A self-described postmodernist, he maintains an intense interest in the stories of "the others" in society. He is currently working on a collection of poems.